HAPPY FEET™

MAD LIBS®

By Roger Price and Leonard Stern

PSS!
PRICE STERN SLOAN

PRICE STERN SLOAN
Published by the Penguin Group
Penguin Group (USA) Inc., 375 Hudson Street, New York, New York 10014, USA
Penguin Group (Canada), 90 Eglinton Avenue East, Suite 700,
Toronto, Ontario, Canada M4P 2Y3
(a division of Pearson Penguin Canada Inc.)
Penguin Books Ltd, 80 Strand, London WC2R 0RL, England
Penguin Ireland, 25 St Stephen's Green, Dublin 2, Ireland (a division of Penguin Books Ltd)
Penguin Group (Australia), 250 Camberwell Road, Camberwell, Victoria 3124, Australia
(a division of Pearson Australia Group Pty Ltd)
Penguin Books India Pvt Ltd, 11 Community Centre,
Panchsheel Park, New Delhi-110 017, India
Penguin Group (NZ), Cnr Airborne and Rosedale Roads,
Albany, Auckland 1310, New Zealand (a division of Pearson New Zealand Ltd)
Penguin Books (South Africa) (Pty) Ltd, 24 Sturdee Avenue,
Rosebank, Johannesburg 2196, South Africa

Penguin Books Ltd, Registered Offices: 80 Strand, London WC2R 0RL, England

Published by Price Stern Sloan,
a division of Penguin Young Readers Group,
345 Hudson Street, New York, New York 10014.

ISBN 0-8431-2093-2

1 3 5 7 9 10 8 6 4 2

MAD LIBS®

INSTRUCTIONS

MAD LIBS® is a game for people who don't like games!
It can be played by one, two, three, four, or forty.

• RIDICULOUSLY SIMPLE DIRECTIONS

In this tablet you will find stories containing blank spaces where words are
left out. One player, the READER, selects one of these stories. The READER
does not tell anyone what the story is about. Instead, he/she asks the other
players, the WRITERS, to give him/her words. These words are used to fil! in
the blank spaces in the story.

• TO PLAY

The READER asks each WRITER in turn to call out a word—an adjective or
a noun or whatever the space calls for—and uses them to fill in the blank
spaces in the story. The result is a MAD LIBS® game.

When the READER then reads the completed MAD LIBS® game to the other
players, they will discover that they have written a story that is fantastic,
screamingly funny, shocking, silly, crazy, or just plain dumb—depending
upon which words each WRITER called out.

• EXAMPLE (*Before and After*)

" _____ !" he said _____
        EXCLAMATION   ADVERB

as he jumped into his convertible _____ and
                                              NOUN

drove off with his _____ wife.
                        ADJECTIVE

" *Ouch* !" he said *stupidly*
        EXCLAMATION   ADVERB

as he jumped into his convertible *cat* and
                                              NOUN

drove off with his *brave* wife.
                        ADJECTIVE

MAD LIBS®

QUICK REVIEW

In case you have forgotten what adjectives, adverbs, nouns, and verbs are, here is a quick review:

An ADJECTIVE describes something or somebody. *Lumpy, soft, ugly, messy,* and *short* are adjectives.

An ADVERB tells how something is done. It modifies a verb and usually ends in "ly." *Modestly, stupidly, greedily,* and *carefully* are adverbs.

A NOUN is the name of a person, place, or thing. *Sidewalk, umbrella, bridle, bathtub,* and *nose* are nouns.

A VERB is an action word. *Run, pitch, jump,* and *swim* are verbs. Put the verbs in past tense if the directions say PAST TENSE. *Ran, pitched, jumped,* and *swam* are verbs in the past tense.

When we ask for A PLACE, we mean any sort of place: a country or city *(Spain, Cleveland)* or a room *(bathroom, kitchen).*

An EXCLAMATION or SILLY WORD is any sort of funny sound, gasp, grunt, or outcry, like *Wow!, Ouch!, Whomp!, Ick!,* and *Gadzooks!*

When we ask for specific words, like a NUMBER, a COLOR, an ANIMAL, or a PART OF THE BODY, we mean a word that is one of those things, like *seven, blue, horse,* or *head*.

When we ask for a PLURAL, it means more than one. For example, *cat* pluralized is *cats*.

MAD LIBS® is fun to play with friends, but you can also play it by yourself! To begin with, DO NOT look at the story on the page below. Fill in the blanks on this page with the words called for. Then, using the words you have selected, fill in the blank spaces in the story.

Now you've created your own hilarious MAD LIBS® game!

MEET MUMBLE

ADVERB _____

NOUN _____

ADJECTIVE _____

NOUN _____

NOUN _____

VERB ENDING IN "ING" _____

ADJECTIVE _____

PART OF THE BODY (PLURAL) _____

ADJECTIVE _____

ADJECTIVE _____

PART OF THE BODY _____

NOUN _____

ADJECTIVE _____

NOUN _____

PLURAL NOUN_____

MAD LIBS
MEET MUMBLE

There's something about Mumble that makes him _____

ADVERB

different from all the other _____ penguins—it is a

NOUN

really _____ problem: He can't sing. Whenever he opens

ADJECTIVE

his _____, it sounds like someone scratching a finger-

NOUN

_____ down a chalkboard or a wolf _____

NOUN   VERB ENDING IN "ING"

at the moon. The noise is so _____ that all the other

ADJECTIVE

penguins have to cover their _____. But Mumble

PART OF THE BODY (PLURAL)

has his own _____ talent—he's a/an _____

ADJECTIVE   ADJECTIVE

dancer. He knows how to put one _____ in front of the

PART OF THE BODY

other and move his _____ to the _____ beat.

NOUN   ADJECTIVE

Mumble is a dancing _____ with those hippity-hoppity

NOUN

_____ of his!

PLURAL NOUN

MAD LIBS® is fun to play with friends, but you can also play it by yourself! To begin with, DO NOT look at the story on the page below. Fill in the blanks on this page with the words called for. Then, using the words you have selected, fill in the blank spaces in the story.

Now you've created your own hilarious MAD LIBS® game!

LOVEBIRDS

PLURAL NOUN _____

PLURAL NOUN _____

NOUN _____

NOUN _____

ADJECTIVE _____

NOUN _____

PLURAL NOUN _____

ADJECTIVE _____

PLURAL NOUN _____

VERB ENDING IN "ING" _____

PLURAL NOUN _____

VERB ENDING IN "ING" _____

MAD LIBS
LOVEBIRDS

Norma Jean and Memphis are Mumble's loving _____.

PLURAL NOUN

They found each other in a large crowd of _____

PLURAL NOUN

and instantly fell in love. Memphis adored the giggle in Norma

Jean's _____, and Norma Jean loved the wiggle in

NOUN

Memphis's _____. But don't let this _____

NOUN   ADJECTIVE

romance fool you—it's not easy for penguins to meet their true

_____. First, they must brave Antarctica's harsh ice and

NOUN

fierce _____. Then they have to find a/an _____

PLURAL NOUN   ADJECTIVE

match to their Heart_____. It's no wonder that

PLURAL NOUN

penguins have to identify one another by their _____,

VERB ENDING IN "ING"

because they all look alike! And when two penguins finally do meet,

they don't have much time together. Someone's always leaving to

look for _____ in the ocean. Maybe they should start a

PLURAL NOUN

penguin _____ service!

VERB ENDING IN "ING"

MAD LIBS® is fun to play with friends, but you can also play it by yourself! To begin with, DO NOT look at the story on the page below. Fill in the blanks on this page with the words called for. Then, using the words you have selected, fill in the blank spaces in the story.

Now you've created your own hilarious MAD LIBS® game!

ALL ABOUT ANTARCTICA

VERB _____

ADJECTIVE _____

ADJECTIVE _____

PLURAL NOUN_____

VERB ENDING IN "ING" _____

ADJECTIVE _____

PLURAL NOUN_____

PLURAL NOUN_____

ADJECTIVE _____

PLURAL NOUN_____

NOUN _____

PLURAL NOUN_____

PLURAL NOUN_____

ADJECTIVE _____

MAD LIBS®
ALL ABOUT ANTARCTICA

The penguins of Happy Feet __spit__ on the continent
VERB

of Antarctica, where the South Pole is located. Ice covers 98

percent of this __slimey__ continent. There are many
ADJECTIVE

__wet__ types of __hair__ __singing__
ADJECTIVE   PLURAL NOUN   VERB ENDING IN "ING"

in Antarctica. Among the species are __clumsy__
ADJECTIVE

penguins, killer __words__, Leopard __cookies__,
PLURAL NOUN   PLURAL NOUN

and a/an __stupid__ variety of __pots__
ADJECTIVE   PLURAL NOUN

that fly in the sky. Antarctica also holds the record for the

coldest __mushroom__ ever recorded—129 __kites__
NOUN   PLURAL NOUN

below zero! Thank goodness the Emperor penguins have

thick __cats__ to protect them from this
PLURAL NOUN

__really small__ cold!
ADJECTIVE

MAD LIBS® is fun to play with friends, but you can also play it by yourself! To begin with, DO NOT look at the story on the page below. Fill in the blanks on this page with the words called for. Then, using the words you have selected, fill in the blank spaces in the story.

Now you've created your own hilarious MAD LIBS® game!

PENGUIN SCHOOL

PLURAL NOUN _____

VERB _____

SILLY WORD _____

SILLY WORD _____

PLURAL NOUN _____

PLURAL NOUN _____

NOUN _____

PLURAL NOUN _____

ADJECTIVE _____

VERB _____

PLURAL NOUN _____

PLURAL NOUN _____

NOUN _____

ADJECTIVE _____

PLURAL NOUN _____

MAD LIBS
PENGUIN SCHOOL

The most important lesson baby _____ learn in penguin
                                    PLURAL NOUN

school is how to find their Heartsongs and _____ them. They
                                              VERB

spend a lot of time singing tra-la-_____ and doobie-doobie-
                                   SILLY WORD

_____. But there are other lessons, too, like learning their
   SILLY WORD

A, B, _____ and their 1, 2, _____. Miss Viola, the
        PLURAL NOUN   PLURAL NOUN

elementary school _____, teaches the little penguins how
                        NOUN

to clean their feathers with their _____. "A good penguin
                                      PLURAL NOUN

is a/an _____ penguin," she says. And the penguins also
          ADJECTIVE

learn how to _____. Miss Viola shows them how to use
                  VERB

their _____ and kick with their _____. Then
       PLURAL NOUN   PLURAL NOUN

she shows them the easiest way to catch a/an _____. And
                                                   NOUN

then there's the most _____ lesson of all—don't eat yellow
                          ADJECTIVE

_____!
   PLURAL NOUN

FROM HAPPY FEET™ MAD LIBS® • Copyright © 2006 Warner Bros. Entertainment Inc. Published by Price
Stern Sloan, a division of Penguin Young Readers Group, 345 Hudson Street, New York, New York 10014.

MAD LIBS® is fun to play with friends, but you can also play it by yourself! To begin with, DO NOT look at the story on the page below. Fill in the blanks on this page with the words called for. Then, using the words you have selected, fill in the blank spaces in the story.

Now you've created your own hilarious MAD LIBS® game!

WHY GLORIA LIKES MUMBLE

ADJECTIVE _____

NOUN _____

ADJECTIVE _____

ADJECTIVE _____

PLURAL NOUN _____

ADJECTIVE _____

NOUN _____

ADJECTIVE _____

PLURAL NOUN _____

MAD LIBS
WHY GLORIA LIKES MUMBLE

Why does Gloria have such _____ feelings for Mumble?
                              ADJECTIVE

Gloria sings as sweetly as a/an _____, and Mumble
                                       NOUN

can't sing a note. The rest of the penguins think Mumble is

_____, but not Gloria. She thinks he is just _____.
   ADJECTIVE   ADJECTIVE

She sings her best when Mumble is tapping his _____. But
                                                 PLURAL NOUN

that's not why Gloria likes Mumble. She likes him because he always

does _____ things for her—like the time he caught a/an
       ADJECTIVE

_____ and gave it to her to eat. It might not have
      NOUN

been obvious at first, but Gloria always knew it—Mumble is a/an

_____ catch! Sometimes _____ really do attract!
   ADJECTIVE   PLURAL NOUN

FROM HAPPY FEET™ MAD LIBS® • Copyright © 2006 Warner Bros. Entertainment Inc. Published by Price
Stern Sloan, a division of Penguin Young Readers Group, 345 Hudson Street, New York, New York 10014.

MAD LIBS® is fun to play with friends, but you can also play it by yourself! To begin with, DO NOT look at the story on the page below. Fill in the blanks on this page with the words called for. Then, using the words you have selected, fill in the blank spaces in the story.

Now you've created your own hilarious MAD LIBS® game!

PENGUIN FACTS

ADJECTIVE _____

PLURAL NOUN _____

PLURAL NOUN _____

ADJECTIVE _____

PLURAL NOUN _____

ADJECTIVE _____

VERB _____

PLURAL NOUN _____

PLURAL NOUN _____

PLURAL NOUN _____

ADVERB _____

NOUN _____

PLURAL NOUN _____

MAD LIBS
PENGUIN FACTS

Here are some _____ little-known facts about penguins:
ADJECTIVE

1) Emperor penguins can be as tall as 3.7 _____ and as
PLURAL NOUN

heavy as ninety _____.
PLURAL NOUN

2) Emperor penguins are the largest of seventeen species, which

also include the _____ Adelies and the Rockhopper
ADJECTIVE

_____.
PLURAL NOUN

3) Penguins are found all over the _____ hemisphere, but
ADJECTIVE

the Emperors, Adelies, and Rockhoppers _____ only in
VERB

Antarctica.

4) All penguins have webbed _____ and small
PLURAL NOUN

_____ instead of wings. Although they are flightless
PLURAL NOUN

_____, they use their flippers to swim _____
PLURAL NOUN   ADVERB

fast.

5) Penguins can hold their _____ underwater from fifteen
NOUN

to twenty _____.
PLURAL NOUN

MAD LIBS® is fun to play with friends, but you can also play it by yourself! To begin with, DO NOT look at the story on the page below. Fill in the blanks on this page with the words called for. Then, using the words you have selected, fill in the blank spaces in the story.

Now you've created your own hilarious MAD LIBS® game!

MRS. ASTRAKHAN'S JOURNAL

NOUN _____

NOUN _____

VERB _____

PLURAL NOUN_____

EXCLAMATION _____

PART OF THE BODY (PLURAL) _____

NOUN _____

NOUN _____

ADJECTIVE _____

NOUN _____

PLURAL NOUN_____

NOUN _____

NOUN _____

Today I met ze leetle pengvin without a/an _____.
                                                              NOUN

Miss Viola sent him to me because I am ze greatest _____
                                                              NOUN

in all of Emperor Land. "No problem," I told her. "Vhen I feenish with

this leetle pengvin, not only vill he know how to _____ but
                                                           VERB

he vill also be givenk everyone the goose-_____." But
                                                   PLURAL NOUN

_____! I failed—he can't sink a note. All he vants to do
   EXCLAMATION

is tap his _____. How vill he ever find a/an
              PART OF THE BODY (PLURAL)

_____ doing that? I was so upset, I banged my head
       NOUN

against a/an _____! All I vant is for the leetle pengvin
                   NOUN

to be _____ and have a good _____, but
         ADJECTIVE   NOUN

with that jiggery-jogging of his _____, how can he?
                                       PLURAL NOUN

Such a catastroff for such a cute leetle _____. Hopefully,
                                                   NOUN

he vill still find his _____.
                          NOUN

FROM HAPPY FEET™ MAD LIBS® • Copyright © 2006 Warner Bros. Entertainment Inc. Published by Price
Stern Sloan, a division of Penguin Young Readers Group, 345 Hudson Street, New York, New York 10014.

MAD LIBS® is fun to play with friends, but you can also play it by yourself! To begin with, DO NOT look at the story on the page below. Fill in the blanks on this page with the words called for. Then, using the words you have selected, fill in the blank spaces in the story.

Now you've created your own hilarious MAD LIBS® game!

SKUA TALK

PERSON IN ROOM _____

PERSON IN ROOM _____

NOUN _____

NOUN _____

PLURAL NOUN _____

PLURAL NOUN _____

VERB _____

VERB ENDING IN "ING" _____

ADJECTIVE _____

NOUN _____

NOUN _____

MAD LIBS®
SKUA TALK

(To be read by _____ as Skua 1 and _____
PERSON IN ROOM　　　　　　　　　　　　　PERSON IN ROOM

as Skua 2.)

Skua 1: Whenever we're just about to eat a yummy _____,
　　　　　　　　　　　　　　　　　　　　　　　　　NOUN

dat skua with de _____ on his leg always messes it up for us.
　　　　　　　　　　NOUN

Skua 2: You can't take dat guy anywhere. All he wants to do is talk

about when he was abducted, an' dose beings with flat, flabby

_____ an' frontways _____.
　PLURAL NOUN　　　　　　　　　PLURAL NOUN

Skua 1: It's embarrasin'. All I want to do is _____, an' I
　　　　　　　　　　　　　　　　　　　　　　　VERB

got dis guy blabbin' away like he's impoitant or somet'in'. It ruins my

appetite.

Skua 2: I'm glad you said somet'in'. I don't think we should go

_____ with him anymore. If he's so _____,
VERB ENDING IN "ING"　　　　　　　　　　　　　　ADJECTIVE

he can find his own meal.

Skua 1: Awright. You hungry? I'm so hungry, I could eat a/an

_____.
　NOUN

Skua 2: You said it. Let's go find us a/an _____ for dinner.
　　　　　　　　　　　　　　　　　　　　　　NOUN

MAD LIBS® is fun to play with friends, but you can also play it by yourself! To begin with, DO NOT look at the story on the page below. Fill in the blanks on this page with the words called for. Then, using the words you have selected, fill in the blank spaces in the story.

Now you've created your own hilarious MAD LIBS® game!

MUMBLE IN ADELIE LAND

NOUN _____

NOUN _____

ADJECTIVE _____

PART OF THE BODY (PLURAL) _____

ADJECTIVE _____

PLURAL NOUN_____

PLURAL NOUN_____

NOUN _____

PLURAL NOUN_____

ADJECTIVE _____

ADJECTIVE _____

PLURAL NOUN_____

VERB ENDING IN "ING" _____

ADJECTIVE _____

VERB _____

ADJECTIVE _____

NOUN _____

MAD LIBS
MUMBLE IN ADELIE LAND

All I was trying to do was escape the _____ seal,

NOUN

when I landed on the shore of Adelie Land. It was the luckiest

_____ of my _____ life. Right in front of
NOUN   ADJECTIVE

my _____ were _____ little penguins
PART OF THE BODY (PLURAL)   ADJECTIVE

playing _____, carrying _____, and dancing to
PLURAL NOUN   PLURAL NOUN

a/an _____ beat. I met these great _____ who
NOUN   PLURAL NOUN

thought I was so _____. Wow! And they loved my
ADJECTIVE

_____ feet! Double wow! The *chicas* and the Amigos
ADJECTIVE

couldn't get enough of my _____ and wanted to start
PLURAL NOUN

_____, too! It is so different from Emperor Land,
VERB ENDING IN "ING"

where no one likes that I am _____ or that I can't
ADJECTIVE

_____. But now that I'm at the head of the conga line,
VERB

things couldn't be more _____! I'm as happy as a bug in
ADJECTIVE

a/an _____.
NOUN

FROM HAPPY FEET™ MAD LIBS® • Copyright © 2006 Warner Bros. Entertainment Inc. Published by Price
Stern Sloan, a division of Penguin Young Readers Group, 345 Hudson Street, New York, New York 10014.

MAD LIBS® is fun to play with friends, but you can also play it by yourself! To begin with, DO NOT look at the story on the page below. Fill in the blanks on this page with the words called for. Then, using the words you have selected, fill in the blank spaces in the story.

Now you've created your own hilarious MAD LIBS® game!

ADELIESPEAK

ADJECTIVE _____

VERB _____

PLURAL NOUN _____

NOUN _____

PLURAL NOUN _____

ADJECTIVE _____

NOUN _____

ADJECTIVE _____

NOUN _____

NOUN _____

VERB _____

NOUN _____

ADJECTIVE _____

VERB _____

PLURAL NOUN _____

NOUN _____

MAD LIBS®
ADELIESPEAK

Do you want to be _____ and _____ just like the
                        ADJECTIVE   VERB

Amigos? It's easy! First, you must give your group of _____
                                                              PLURAL NOUN

nicknames. The Amigos call Mumble "Tall _____"
                                                    NOUN

or "Fluffy" to make him feel like one of the _____. You
                                                      PLURAL NOUN

could even give yourself a/an _____ nickname like "Cool
                                      ADJECTIVE

_____" or "_____ Dude." And when you want
        NOUN   ADJECTIVE

to congratulate or compliment a friend or a/an _____,
                                                          NOUN

you just say, "You're the _____, hombre" or "Way to
                                  NOUN

_____." It's always nice to get a/an _____
        VERB   NOUN

on the back, and it's important to let your friends know how

_____ they are. Just _____ as the Amigos do and
    ADJECTIVE   VERB

you're bound to win _____ and be the _____ of
                          PLURAL NOUN   NOUN

the party!

MAD LIBS® is fun to play with friends, but you can also play it by yourself! To begin with, DO NOT look at the story on the page below. Fill in the blanks on this page with the words called for. Then, using the words you have selected, fill in the blank spaces in the story.

Now you've created your own hilarious MAD LIBS® game!

RAMON'S GUIDE TO BEING COOL

NOUN _____

PLURAL NOUN _____

ADJECTIVE _____

NOUN _____

ADJECTIVE _____

PART OF THE BODY (PLURAL) _____

NOUN _____

PLURAL NOUN _____

ADJECTIVE _____

VERB _____

NOUN _____

MAD LIBS®
RAMON'S GUIDE TO BEING COOL

Everyone's always asking me, "Ramon, how'd you get to be so cool?"

What can I say? I can't help being the ______________ everybody
NOUN

wants. Nothing ever ruffles my ______________. I'm always
PLURAL NOUN

______________ with the ladies, a real man's ______________, and I'm
ADJECTIVE NOUN

as close to perfect as penguinly possible. So how do I do it, amigos?

It's actually very ______________—you jus' gotta be true to yourself.
ADJECTIVE

That's why my main *muchacho*, Mumble, is ______________
PART OF THE BODY (PLURAL)

down the coolest ______________ in the Southern Hemisphere
NOUN

(second only to me, of course). No matter how many ______________
PLURAL NOUN

it costs him, he never tries to be someone he's not. So if you want to

be ______________, just ______________ as I do (or Mumble does)
ADJECTIVE VERB

and you'll always be one cool ______________.
NOUN

MAD LIBS® is fun to play with friends, but you can also play it by yourself! To begin with, DO NOT look at the story on the page below. Fill in the blanks on this page with the words called for. Then, using the words you have selected, fill in the blank spaces in the story.

Now you've created your own hilarious MAD LIBS® game!

LOVELACE HAS THE ANSWERS

PLURAL NOUN _____

ADJECTIVE _____

ADJECTIVE _____

PLURAL NOUN _____

NOUN _____

NOUN _____

NOUN _____

NOUN _____

NOUN _____

ADJECTIVE _____

PLURAL NOUN _____

PLURAL NOUN _____

PLURAL NOUN _____

MAD LIBS®
LOVELACE HAS THE ANSWERS

Ladies and _____, this is your _____ day.
             PLURAL NOUN   ADJECTIVE

I, Lovelace the Guru, will tell you how I use my _____
                                                         ADJECTIVE

powers to contact the Mystic _____. Just bring a/an
                                        PLURAL NOUN

_____ in your beak and a question to ask. But remember:
     NOUN

one pebble, one _____! Throughout the years, penguins
                       NOUN

have come to me asking all sorts of questions, like "Will I ever find

my one true _____?" "Will I ever win the _____?"
               NOUN   NOUN

and even "Why are we living on this _____?" On rare
                                  NOUN

occasions, I am asked by a/an _____ disbeliever if I truly
                             ADJECTIVE

have magical _____. Let's just say that thanks to my special
             PLURAL NOUN

_____, I've got enough _____ in my pile to last
  PLURAL NOUN   PLURAL NOUN

me a lifetime!

MAD LIBS® is fun to play with friends, but you can also play it by yourself! To begin with, DO NOT look at the story on the page below. Fill in the blanks on this page with the words called for. Then, using the words you have selected, fill in the blank spaces in the story.

Now you've created your own hilarious MAD LIBS® game!

WHAT THE LADIES LIKE ABOUT LOVELACE

PLURAL NOUN_____

SAME PLURAL NOUN _____

PLURAL NOUN_____

ADJECTIVE _____

NOUN _____

PLURAL NOUN_____

ADJECTIVE _____

NOUN _____

NOUN _____

PLURAL NOUN_____

MAD LIBS®
WHAT THE LADIES
LIKE ABOUT LOVELACE

Why do the ladies love Lovelace? He has more _____

PLURAL NOUN

than any other penguin. With those _____ he can

SAME PLURAL NOUN

make the best nests for little _____. And then there's his

PLURAL NOUN

_____ fashion sense. Those rings around his neck make him

ADJECTIVE

look like the _____'s pajamas. And the ladies just love the

NOUN

way all the other penguins look up to Lovelace and ask him for the

_____ to their most important questions. It's all because

PLURAL NOUN

Lovelace has _____ powers that have been bestowed upon

ADJECTIVE

him by the Mystic Beings. What a/an _____! Lovelace is the

NOUN

life of the party, the king of the _____, and an all-around

NOUN

_____' man.

PLURAL NOUN

FROM HAPPY FEET™ MAD LIBS® • Copyright © 2006 Warner Bros. Entertainment Inc. Published by Price
Stern Sloan, a division of Penguin Young Readers Group, 345 Hudson Street, New York, New York 10014.

MAD LIBS® is fun to play with friends, but you can also play it by yourself! To begin with, DO NOT look at the story on the page below. Fill in the blanks on this page with the words called for. Then, using the words you have selected, fill in the blank spaces in the story.

Now you've created your own hilarious MAD LIBS® game!

THE AMIGOS' GUIDE
TO LOOOVE

PLURAL NOUN _____

PLURAL NOUN _____

SAME PLURAL NOUN _____

PART OF THE BODY _____

PLURAL NOUN _____

ADVERB _____

VERB _____

ADJECTIVE _____

NOUN _____

PLURAL NOUN _____

NOUN _____

ADVERB _____

PLURAL NOUN _____

NOUN _____

PART OF THE BODY (PLURAL) _____

MAD LIBS®
THE AMIGOS' GUIDE TO LOOOVE

So, *muchachos*, you want to be a/an _____' man like us,
<u>PLURAL NOUN</u>

the Amigos? Then here's what you have to do. In order to impress

your lady, you have to collect as many _____ as possible.
<u>PLURAL NOUN</u>

The more _____ you give her, the better your chances
<u>SAME PLURAL NOUN</u>

of winning her _____. To really knock your lady off
<u>PART OF THE BODY</u>

her _____, you must do something _____
<u>PLURAL NOUN</u>   <u>ADVERB</u>

sensational. Perhaps you can _____ like Mumble, or you
<u>VERB</u>

have a/an _____ singing _____ like Nestor. Or
<u>ADJECTIVE</u>   <u>NOUN</u>

maybe you're just lucky to have the *chicas* falling at your webbed

_____, like Lovelace. Still, you must always treat your
<u>PLURAL NOUN</u>

_____ _____. If you play your _____
<u>NOUN</u>   <u>ADVERB</u>   <u>PLURAL NOUN</u>

right, you'll have every _____ drooling at your
<u>NOUN</u>

_____!
<u>PART OF THE BODY (PLURAL)</u>

FROM HAPPY FEET™ MAD LIBS® • Copyright © 2006 Warner Bros. Entertainment Inc. Published by Price
Stern Sloan, a division of Penguin Young Readers Group, 345 Hudson Street, New York, New York 10014.

MAD LIBS® is fun to play with friends, but you can also play it by yourself! To begin with, DO NOT look at the story on the page below. Fill in the blanks on this page with the words called for. Then, using the words you have selected, fill in the blank spaces in the story.

Now you've created your own hilarious MAD LIBS® game!

HOW TO TAP-DANCE . . . ON ICE!

NOUN _____

ADVERB _____

PART OF THE BODY _____

NOUN _____

TYPE OF LIQUID_____

PART OF THE BODY _____

VERB _____

PLURAL NOUN_____

PLURAL NOUN_____

PLURAL NOUN_____

MAD LIBS®
HOW TO TAP-DANCE...
ON ICE!

Mumble makes tap dancing on ice look like __hippo__'s play,
NOUN

but it's really very hard. You always have to be __quickly__
ADVERB

careful not to slip. You could land right on your __toe__
PART OF THE BODY

or fall flat on your __cat__, or worse yet, you could fall
NOUN

off a cliff and land in the freezing __milk__ below. Talk
TYPE OF LIQUID

about embarrassing! You wouldn't be able to show your

__bellybutton__ around for a long time. So to avoid any
PART OF THE BODY

dancing disasters, __jump__ on the __tous__ instead
VERB   PLURAL NOUN

of on the ice, rub __pens__ on your feet, and always be
PLURAL NOUN

careful of where you put your __hair__!
PLURAL NOUN

FROM HAPPY FEET™ MAD LIBS® • Copyright © 2006 Warner Bros. Entertainment Inc. Published by Price Stern Sloan, a division of Penguin Young Readers Group, 345 Hudson Street, New York, New York 10014.

MAD LIBS® is fun to play with friends, but you can also play it by yourself! To begin with, DO NOT look at the story on the page below. Fill in the blanks on this page with the words called for. Then, using the words you have selected, fill in the blank spaces in the story.

Now you've created your own hilarious MAD LIBS® game!

ALL ABOUT ELEPHANT SEALS

ADJECTIVE _____

NOUN _____

PLURAL NOUN_____

PLURAL NOUN_____

ADJECTIVE _____

PLURAL NOUN_____

VERB _____

PLURAL NOUN_____

VERB ENDING IN "ING"_____

NOUN _____

VERB ENDING IN "ING" _____

PART OF THE BODY (PLURAL) _____

MAD LIBS®
ALL ABOUT ELEPHANT SEALS

On their way to the Forbidden Shore, Mumble and the gang met

up with a group of _____ elephant seals resting by the
ADJECTIVE

_____. They're named elephant seals because the males
NOUN

have tusks coming out of their _____, just like the
PLURAL NOUN

_____ in Africa and Asia. Slow and _____ on
PLURAL NOUN   ADJECTIVE

land but fast _____ in the sea, elephant seals love to
PLURAL NOUN

_____ in the water. Even though they are _____,
VERB   PLURAL NOUN

elephant seals can go without _____ underwater
VERB ENDING IN "ING"

for almost two hours! They also love to soak up the _____.
NOUN

Sometimes you can find hundreds of them _____
VERB ENDING IN "ING"

on the beach at the same time! The males can grow up to twenty

_____ and weigh up to four tons. No wonder the
PART OF THE BODY (PLURAL)

little penguins kept their distance!

FROM HAPPY FEET™ MAD LIBS® • Copyright © 2006 Warner Bros. Entertainment Inc. Published by Price
Stern Sloan, a division of Penguin Young Readers Group, 345 Hudson Street, New York, New York 10014.

MAD LIBS® is fun to play with friends, but you can also play it by yourself! To begin with, DO NOT look at the story on the page below. Fill in the blanks on this page with the words called for. Then, using the words you have selected, fill in the blank spaces in the story.

Now you've created your own hilarious MAD LIBS® game!

HOW TO CATCH A FISH

NOUN _____

NOUN _____

TYPE OF LIQUID_____

PLURAL NOUN_____

ADJECTIVE _____

NOUN _____

PLURAL NOUN_____

PLURAL NOUN_____

ADJECTIVE _____

NOUN _____

ADJECTIVE _____

VERB _____

NOUN _____

PLURAL NOUN_____

MAD LIBS®
HOW TO CATCH A FISH

Now that there are plenty of fish in the ocean again, some of you

need to relearn how to catch a/an __meat__ . Take a deep
                                      NOUN

__fork__ before diving into the deep blue __cake__ .
  NOUN   TYPE OF LIQUID

The deeper you go, the better the __pillows__ you'll find.
                                    PLURAL NOUN

But be ready for a/an __stinky__ chase—some underwater
                        ADJECTIVE

creatures can travel faster than a speeding __dog__ . You also
                                              NOUN

have to be careful of which __fingers__ you catch. Those big
                              PLURAL NOUN

__pigs__ might look __noisey__ and seem like they
  PLURAL NOUN   ADJECTIVE

could feed an entire __eye__ , but watch out—they're much
                       NOUN

too __shiney__ for any one penguin to __lick__ . And
     ADJECTIVE   VERB

always remember to come up for a big breath every once in a while.

You certainly won't be able to catch a/an __book__ without
                                            NOUN

any air in your __sequins__ .
                 PLURAL NOUN

MAD LIBS® is fun to play with friends, but you can also play it by yourself! To begin with, DO NOT look at the story on the page below. Fill in the blanks on this page with the words called for. Then, using the words you have selected, fill in the blank spaces in the story.

Now you've created your own hilarious MAD LIBS® game!

THE ELDERS' NEW RULES

NOUN _____

PLURAL NOUN_____

PLURAL NOUN_____

ADJECTIVE _____

PLURAL NOUN_____

ADJECTIVE _____

NOUN _____

PLURAL NOUN_____

ADJECTIVE _____

NOUN _____

ADJECTIVE _____

ADVERB _____

VERB ENDING IN "ING" _____

ADJECTIVE _____

NOUN _____

MAD LIBS®
THE ELDERS' NEW RULES

Boy, were we wrong about Mumble! It turns out that he wasn't a/an

_____ at all—he brought back the _____ and
　　　NOUN　　　　　　　　　　　　　　　　　　　PLURAL NOUN

saved the emperor _____. To make sure something like
　　　　　　　　　PLURAL NOUN

this never happens again, we're going to make some _____
　　　　　　　　　　　　　　　　　　　　　　　　　　ADJECTIVE

changes around here. We hope that with these new _____
　　　　　　　　　　　　　　　　　　　　　　　　　　PLURAL NOUN

Emperor Land will be a lot more _____ and certainly more
　　　　　　　　　　　　　　　　　ADJECTIVE

fun for every _____!
　　　　　　　　NOUN

1) From this day forward, Emperor Land will accept a diversity of

_____ into its _____ community. It doesn't
　PLURAL NOUN　　　　　　　ADJECTIVE

matter how a penguin expresses his or her Heart_____,
　　　　　　　　　　　　　　　　　　　　　　　　NOUN

just as long as the little penguin is _____.
　　　　　　　　　　　　　　　　　　ADJECTIVE

2) Dance classes will start _____. You can sign up for tap,
　　　　　　　　　　　　　　　ADVERB

jazz, or modern _____. Mumble, our _____
　　　　　　　　VERB ENDING IN "ING"　　　　　　　ADJECTIVE

friend, has even volunteered to be the class _____!
　　　　　　　　　　　　　　　　　　　　　　NOUN

MAD LIBS® is fun to play with friends, but you can also play it by yourself! To begin with, DO NOT look at the story on the page below. Fill in the blanks on this page with the words called for. Then, using the words you have selected, fill in the blank spaces in the story.

Now you've created your own hilarious MAD LIBS® game!

MUMBLE'S MANY HAPPY FEET

VERB _____

SILLY WORD _____

VERB ENDING IN "ING" _____

NOUN _____

PLURAL NOUN _____

NOUN _____

ADJECTIVE _____

VERB ENDING IN "ING" _____

PLURAL NOUN _____

VERB ENDING IN "ING" _____

PLURAL NOUN _____

MAD LIBS
MUMBLE'S MANY HAPPY FEET

Mumble loves to tap _____ and hear the _____-
                         VERB   SILLY WORD

click-click of his feet. But did you know that Mumble loves other

types of dancing, too? He and Gloria love _____
                                              VERB ENDING IN "ING"

to the salsa _____ and tangoing across the ice with
                  NOUN

_____ in their beaks. Mumble also loves to leap across
   PLURAL NOUN

the ice like a ballet _____. And when Seymour starts
                           NOUN

rapping, Mumble can't stop grooving to the _____ beat.
                                                ADJECTIVE

He and the Amigos always have fun _____ in a
                                       VERB ENDING IN "ING"

conga line and kicking their _____. Mumble will always love
                                PLURAL NOUN

tap dancing most, but he knows that it's good to try new ways of

_____. You never know how much fun you might
  VERB ENDING IN "ING"

have or what new _____ you'll discover!
                     PLURAL NOUN

FROM HAPPY FEET™ MAD LIBS® • Copyright © 2006 Warner Bros. Entertainment Inc. Published by Price
Stern Sloan, a division of Penguin Young Readers Group, 345 Hudson Street, New York, New York 10014.

MAD LIBS® is fun to play with friends, but you can also play it by yourself! To begin with, DO NOT look at the story on the page below. Fill in the blanks on this page with the words called for. Then, using the words you have selected, fill in the blank spaces in the story.

Now you've created your own hilarious MAD LIBS® game!

FILL IN A HEARTSONG

ADJECTIVE _____

VERB ENDING IN "ING" _____

ADJECTIVE _____

ADJECTIVE _____

NOUN _____

ADJECTIVE _____

NOUN _____

NOUN _____

NOUN _____

ADJECTIVE _____

NOUN _____

VERB _____

VERB _____

NOUN _____

NOUN _____

MAD LIBS
FILL IN A HEARTSONG

Most of the time I feel _____.
ADJECTIVE

I'm _____ and having a/an _____ time.
VERB ENDING IN "ING"   ADJECTIVE

But there are times when I'm so _____,
ADJECTIVE

and the only thing that can cure me is your _____.
NOUN

I searched high and _____ for you, baby-_____.
ADJECTIVE   NOUN

You are my _____ in the dark and my _____
NOUN   NOUN

in the rain.

I want to spend my _____ _____ with you.
ADJECTIVE   NOUN

When you _____, I can't help but smile,
VERB

and your laugh always makes me _____.
VERB

I was made for your _____, and you were made for my
NOUN

_____!
NOUN

FROM HAPPY FEET™ MAD LIBS® • Copyright © 2006 Warner Bros. Entertainment Inc. Published by Price
Stern Sloan, a division of Penguin Young Readers Group, 345 Hudson Street, New York, New York 10014.

MAD LIBS® is fun to play with friends, but you can also play it by yourself! To begin with, DO NOT look at the story on the page below. Fill in the blanks on this page with the words called for. Then, using the words you have selected, fill in the blank spaces in the story.

Now you've created your own hilarious MAD LIBS® game!

MUMBLE'S BIG PERFORMANCE

ADJECTIVE _____

NOUN _____

ADJECTIVE _____

PLURAL NOUN _____

VERB _____

NOUN _____

PLURAL NOUN _____

ADVERB _____

NOUN _____

VERB ENDING IN "ING" _____

SILLY WORD _____

ADVERB _____

NOUN _____

PLURAL NOUN _____

ADJECTIVE _____

VERB _____

VERB (PAST TENSE) _____

NOUN _____

NOUN _____

MAD LIBS
MUMBLE'S BIG PERFORMANCE

It was a/an _____ night. The southern lights lit up
                    ADJECTIVE

the _____. All the Emperor penguins were feeling
              NOUN

_____—the _____ were back in the
    ADJECTIVE   PLURAL NOUN

ocean. Suddenly, a group of penguins started to _____,
                                                        VERB

and Mumble appeared on the _____. He began tapping
                                    NOUN

his _____ to the beat. Then he moved _____
        PLURAL NOUN   ADVERB

all over the _____. Soon everyone was _____
                  NOUN   VERB ENDING IN "ING"

along with Mumble. "_____!" they shouted _____.
                        SILLY WORD   ADVERB

Then a special guest _____ appeared beside Mumble—
                            NOUN

it was Gloria! "Move those _____ and sing a/an
                                PLURAL NOUN

_____ song," Mumble cried out to her. Gloria began to
    ADJECTIVE

_____ and Mumble _____ even better!
    VERB   VERB (PAST TENSE)

The two penguins brought down the _____. It was a/an
                                        NOUN

_____ to remember!
    NOUN

FROM HAPPY FEET™ MAD LIBS® • Copyright © 2006 Warner Bros. Entertainment Inc. Published by Price
Stern Sloan, a division of Penguin Young Readers Group, 345 Hudson Street, New York, New York 10014.